Lullabies
for the
Impatient

Howard Barker

Lullabies for the Impatient

JOHN CALDER : LONDON
RIVERRUN PRESS : NEW YORK

First published in Great Britain, 1988, by
John Calder (Publishers) Ltd.,
18, Brewer Street, London W1R 4AS

and in the United States of America, 1988, by
Riverrun Press Inc
1170 Broadway
New York, NY 10010

British Library Cataloguing in Publication Data

Barker, Howard, 1946-
Lullabies for the impatient
1. Title
821'.914
ISBN 0—7145—4153—2

Printed in Great Britain by Delta Press, Hove.
Typeset in Baskerville by Oxford University Computing Service.

To Jo
For his company

We fail to think correctly
There is the hope
We persist in our blindness
There is the hope
We are intransigent at the wrong moment
And capitulate at the wrong moment
There is the sole chance of deliverance

(Preface to the Radio version of
The Possibilities).

Contents

Chelmno

The Castle

I am the English watercolourist
Arthur Taylor
Born 1820
Skilled
But

Finding the market for the
Picturesque saturated and my
Talent dwarfed I took the
Steamer

And by a multitude of carriages
And haywains I have reached
Galicia

A level and unlikely landscape
To test the tolerance of my
Medium in this impoverished light

How silent these estates
And lacking walls
How unregulated the paths
And gateless

While hedges which characterize
My rural views
Have no relations here

I have much to learn
I have much to forget
Much I must look for
Much I must not expect

The problem for the painter here
Is to discover the necessary form
The object which commands the eye
The irresistible perspective

Having chosen to travel East
In arbitrary disdain of
More familiar tours
I have already learned
The taste of the majority
Is not uneducated

How I hunger for a cliff
A promontory
Even a road that turns

Who will bid for my portfolio?
They will say these pictures prove
What many of us always thought

That Arthur Taylor lacks
The power of the sublime
He suffers all the weakness
Of the self-taught

Whereupon
Emerging
From
A forest
I beheld

The crenellations
Latticed
And baroque
The pinnacles
The casements
The gate piers
The terraces
The statuary
Skittishly weaving
Among pools
The balusters
The quoins
The fishscaled tiles
Of sham castles

Chelmno
Above the Narew

Inspired by the uninspired
I
Arthur Taylor
Born 1820
With a living to make
And few ideas
Climbed seven flights

My easel lighter
My feet bathed in hope
My mouth primed to exaggerate
My reputation
At the door's first crack

How welcome the libations of a snob!
The count endures the provincial sickness
With the languid fortitude displayed by
Connoisseurs

Only his neck is grimed
And this in spite of plumbing
Brought by wagon from Berlin
Ceramics from Limoges
Basins from Birmingham

Our French is adequate to
Veil my common origins
And cause his loneliness to
Trickle from an effusive lip

I lie freely
And the rooks as if protesting
Scrape their throats
I lay my sketches on his desk
With arcane and pretentious notes

How well I smile
I catch it in a mirror
How it contains the essence of
Arthur Taylor

His talent being such
As to require the props
That charm can lend
And wit attest

Already I am commissioned
To view the castle from both
East and West

To prepare wash drawings
Of the reception rooms
In summer and in winter light

6

And prefigure the landscape
So that he might site
The still uncrated Temple
Of the Winds

He titles me his English Advisant
Asking that I judge the grounds
Their style
Their fashion
And whether he should plant
A grove where Venus rises
Unhealthily from sloven waters

Chelmno
Above the Narew

Which from my rooms in the
Unfurnished wing
Shows the temper of a predator
Not running but stalking
In its banks

At breakfast in a borrowed robe
I demonstrate the techniques
Of my craft
Effusive
Garrulous
He gasps and laughs
At my saturated surfaces

How the salon echoes!
Since the last plasterer left
No lung has boomed here or grin
Dipped the mirror glass

Arthur Taylor
The dispenser of the new
Views Poland from the penthouse
Its swamps
Its forests
Its resentful sky

His face a pale speck
In the march of roofs
His little window
A frail cry

And in the draught's indecent feeling
Of the eaves
His paper limps across vast floors
Of naked wood

Chelmno
Above the Narew

It's time I left
So much approval subtly strains
The will
And the castle will be an unrewarding
Subject until
Some history happens here

Landscape is experience
Landscape is the absent hand
It calls
It summons
The obscure from unrecorded labour
And forgotten crime

It abhors the manufactured
It abhors the bland
Insistent on the print of pains

I
Arthur Taylor
Born 1820
Modestly gifted
And less servile
Than predicted

Pack my colours
Wax my boots
Sign my drawings
Flourish my excuse

How
Terribly
Alone
The
Sensitive
And
Artistic
Are

My patron complains
His lip fringed with breakfast
His cuff mapped with coffee stains

How terribly alone

The liveried serf
Transports my easel to the gates
It is a hard life for the master
He's in debt to the Jew

He waves me up the road

Chelmno
Above the Narew

The Early Hours of a Reviled Man

Practising medicine among the poor
He neglected his appearance
Shaving spasmodically
Smoking in the consulting room
And bearing the marks of their
Sickness on his cuffs

At the closing of the surgery door
He wrote on the prescription pad
Some routine abuse of the Jews
Then ran his hand under the tap.
His wound ached like a hated wife
Coming round from an attack,
It ached like a beaten woman
Climbing off the floor.

The behaviour of flesh endorsed
His principle that suffering
Was the evidence of humour
In the foundation of the world.
He admired the cancer cell for its wit
He admired its stealth
Its refusal to submit.
He discovered in disease the futility
Of both love and contempt.
How he hated the humanists
Their mad and violent symmetry
Their pursuit of justice
Even in the wards!

And on his desk he kept a Laocoon
A fool struggling with irrationality

Taking his stick
He limped the streets
He could not write yet
He never could write
Until they slept
He could not write
Unless it was a crime

It required the illegality
It required the treachery
That came with the hour of theft

How iced this air off the river
And the gambler's laugh is
Innocent as a dropped pin

How iced this air
And the girl dragged under the arch
Makes the sound of water
Brightly leaving the sink

He will walk for fifteen minutes
He will observe the stacking of chairs
The expulsion of the legless
The kisses false yet lavish as desserts

How will he hide when the time comes
How will he shrink?

He will withdraw over a burned landscape
Hating his allies
He will linger in the bombed aisles
Of undistinguished chapels
Wishing it was over
He will laugh
At the catastrophe of cultures
Wishing it was over

And the tracked vehicles will sound
Like pigs in the conveyor

He will fall on his side
And the songs of the liberators
Will pour from their necks
Like beer from shaken bottles

How his old fountain pen sings
How it sings along the lines

All this secret testament
They will tie with ribbon
And his patients will stand
To recall his smile was
Pharmaceutical
His lips thinly spilling the voice
A cracked fountain
In an abandoned yard.

Another Transitional State

The yacht is laughing at the survival
Of its class
Listen
Its pearls rattle along rigging
As the pinnace
Carries the undying wealthy to their berths

My old mother lies in a chemical sleep
One sheet over her body in the heat
And the streetlamp in her mirror
Is a solitary audience

On the wireless a politician wishes
He had perished in the long-forgotten war
How uncomfortable he feels in his grave suit
And his hat is stuffed with handkerchiefs
Wet from extinguished solidarities

A U boat smiles under the sands
Its captain was a poet in trajectories
His sister lies in a room
Dreading the rise of Africa

If only winter would rush in
Waving its weapons
If only the cold would stop
The laughter in the mouth

A man is drifting over the trees
Strapped to an engine
He is no less historic than the pioneers
No less absurd than the innovators

When he strikes the copse
And the broken branch
Pins him like a fly to the thorn
I shall say nothing

For there is nothing to say

As he hangs absurdly
A fatuous Christ in his trunks
I shall look the other way
Reaching for a little alcohol
I shall imagine the perfect life

You
My
Restless
Mistress

You
My
Incorrigible
Wife

You
My
Glimpsed
Infatuation

And the painted cloth of rurality
Will hang behind my mask
It will have the appearance of bliss
It will have the necessary features
Of the perfect evening prior to a war
Whose very fragrance sits
In the memory of the recollectionists

Obviously we are waiting for something
The moth alights
And the leaves are a congregation
Hushed for a single remark

The Hapsburg Barracks, Prague

This grass between the cobbles
This gate unopened sixty years
This monogram above the lintel

Oh, the fatuous faith of dead classes!
With hindsight we can prove
Their oaths were blind!

This rank of vacant windows
This wind of belittling mischief
Plucking rust from the railings

Oh, the misplaced loyalty of cadets!
If only they possessed our tools
Of social analysis!

They trod this pavement laughing
They climbed this hill swaggering
They turned their badges to the sun

Oh, the comic pathos of other men's convictions!
And we so opulent with means
To separate the slogan from the valid!

Five Proofs of Existence

How beautiful my neighbour is
Her face is red as oxides
Quarried from dissenting life
And her legs are wreathed in vein

How softly spoken my neighbour is
Unless I complain
Then her eyes shout and breathlessly
She rebukes me for living alone

How restless my neighbour is
She dreams at the bidding of the sun
Her back is water pouring over a stone
And her ancient blouse is undone

How swift my neighbour is
To be naked in the half-dark room
Her rinsed things chase
Each other to the boards

How educated my neighbour is
She has lived with many men
She knows the shallowness of oaths
And says simply at the hour's end

In

   the

      event

         we

           need

              again

                 tap

2

I write you this love letter
Mother of sons
I fling this shameless utterance
You small-wristed and ill-tempered
You strong and insubstantial
Body of straws and whims

I would have thrown my clothes about
And white gone to your whiteness
In that bed of stillbirth

How your unmasked
How your still and washed of action
Face implored my kisses
Death inside you lending
Certitude at last
And your petulant mouth
For once unstrung

I should have clasped your arse
To my hard hip
And declared myself the husband
Rigid with insolence
In that place of pity

Usurper and pretender
I saw there
In your frank worthlessness
Our love's chance

3

I have laid aside the philosopher
To draw your arse
He talks too emphatically of killing

I have thrown down the slaughterer's manual
To memorize you
My faint breasts masked under linen

If he endorses massacre once more
I shall burn him
I shall see his words roar in the grate
It is not philosophical to give blind hate
Permission
We must demand more of each other

We must demand more of each other
My tragic mouthed one
How your uneven teeth are a fence

Over which my tongue leaps an incensed
Lieutenant
We must turn aside our just blows

4

Here my mistress sits with her red lips
Giving pain to the ineligible

Here her legs make stricken vessels
Of the simply ambitious

Here her voice too loud for modesty
Too articulate for superiority

With jagged syllables attracts the eye
Half-abject and half-criminal

She has not washed for mischief
And her pungency between the hops

Is sensed by sullen husbands who have swopped
Dinners for audacity

How poorly we shall live in our decline
Posturing on crutches

How we shall court contempt believing
Ourselves still powerful

We shall skid on polished floors and lie
Like shot deer stranded

While porters drape our snapped limbs
In unsympathetic cloths

5

She
    lay
        like
            that
                to
                    emphasize
                                abandonment

She
    drowsed
            childishly
                    to
                      indicate
                            other
                                  fatigues

She
    walked
        in
           arid
              fields
                    to
                      invite
                            comparisons

And
    let
        the
           wind's
              hand
                  dispose
                      her
                        knees

Even
    her
        shabbiness
              proclaimed
                  an
                    aching
                        to
                      be
                        prized

On the Sickness of Art Forms

First, those to whom expression was given
Ceased to practice

Second, those to whom power was lent
Preferred applause

Third, the former and the latter combined
To silence the dissonant voice

And the theatre became not a platform
Against which those who had no power
Of description might cling
Empowered and boldened by surprise but

A
  Laughing
        Box
             Descending
                    The
                          Stairs

Falling
      Whole
           Flights
                And
                    Tinkling

Like the Christmas present flung
By the angry postman at the wall

Juxtaposition of a Madman with a
Naval Patrol Boat

Oh heart of hatred you plough the pavement
With boots Indefatigable and Indominitable

Oh head of wild hair you smoke the trees
With signals for offensive action

And your hips cleave the shrinking air
Bows high in the flood of temper

Your white ankles flap admonishments
Fearless and Vindictive

You prickle with the armaments of rage
And your mouth moves with silent oaths

Of loyalty to your monarch Mayhem

Thin Actress

She rings me from Paris
Wondering
She lies curiously in
Her hotel
Ambition fits her tightly
Like a dress
Which cracks noisily to touch
All pleats
Like the flanks of an accordion
Black eyes
Like fast marmosets on bars
She rings me from Paris
Wondering
Have I written her a part
Which will
Create her as her coiled cruelty
Might explain me?

She lies on the hotel bed
And everything
From her infant ankle
To the raging den of her mouth
Anticipates
This mash of our opposed nerves
She rips resistance from the audience
As a cat claws rents
In a glove

She lashes my pitiless
Meaning
To the deck of their seasick
Minds

My Rooms

Impetuous I
Aggrieved I
Enter these rooms as the tongue
Of the madman rushes round his mouth

Aching I
Contemptuous I
Drift these rooms as the dead barge
Booms against the piles of the creek

Afraid I
Besieged I
Dart these rooms as the insect struck
By lamplight hurtles for crevices

Loving I
Proud I
Lap these rooms as a father bathes
His infant in extravagant kisses

I greet these walls whose skin is
Thinly glazed in all my tempers

The Novice's Anticipation of Christ

How fine my wrists appear
Extending from starched cuffs
They show the perfect form of
The mechanical or lying still
Are chaste as tools laid on their edge
And my fingers are ranked accessories.

How taut my neck is and unlined
It emerges from the collar
With the tension of a gull
Rising from still water
And my throat has the odour
And the cruelty of new paper.

How spare my arse feels to my hand
Not rolling with the rhythm
Of the panniered mule
Nor forked with austerity
But expressing under the cloth
The contours of warm charity.

If Christ came I should know Him
By His body's economy
His standing without calculation
His eyes which saw only enough
And His voice of wood on wood
Not carrying beyond the breath.

If Christ invited me to walk
He would observe how I did not
Press questions nor was I diffident
Hearing Him out and lifting the subject
From His discourse deftly as the craftsman
Trowels mortar from the board.

If He woke me at a solitary hour
I should be hollow-eyed and pale as Him
And drawing my knees under my chin
Would look with a critical expression
My long jaw extended in
An attitude of patient mockery.

How coarse and copious my hair is
Rising like an exclamation
If He laid a hand there
I should say nothing neither
Contradicting nor approving
Unsurprised and unrewarded

And when He left me in the morning
I should go naked to the latrines
Outstaring my sisters' stares
I should wash at the wound He had made
And think pitifully of Him
Who had failed to remain essential.

Morning—Democracy with Crows

I skated the furrowed field and the sea stood up
                                                        like a wall
I climbed the bickering fence and the gulls moved
                                                        their mouths

With the pain of offended landowners
Silently as if vocabulary had failed to fire
I greeted the slugs with a roar of affection
And lifted the snail from the path
Before the heel of the athletic broke the solitude
Of this unpopulated hour
I shouted the name of a woman
Who under such a cliff had loved me in a rain
Clumsy and fastidious bold and half-ashamed
I boomed my titles to clouds thin
As old women's hair in the wards
And the crows stood heraldic to me
Nothing was shared
We occupied the undulating space
We did not see things in the same way
We acknowledged
We made no claims

The Return of the Defeated Mercenary to Florence

Significantly it hangs low
The pennant of my lover
A rag in the midst of laughter
My inept prince
Ostentatiously it transports
His humiliation down ranks
Of civic certitude

How
Long
These
Shadows
Are
Cascading over pavements
In the airless afternoon
Scholars might unfold light stools
And murmuring draw veils
Between their charcoal knees
Celibates
And
Dissuaders
And the wives of lawyers

Impeccably bare-legged
From the cool museums
Stare through rinsed retinas
Floribunda
And
Crustacea
Trawl your thin colours
Through their unease
My studiously unclean
My skilfully unshaven
Thief of confidences
Even the wound on your elbow
Was self-inflicted!
How accurately I anticipated
The style of your return
And drew your cynical smile
On back pages of my texts
Unruly schoolgirl

His Funeral

I

I am wearing new shoes
Black leather in which I will
Walk clumsily with hurt heels
I am wearing a white shirt
Pure cotton to catch
The winter light
Never do I wear black shoes
Or shirts in white
You see what I do for you
You see what your death
Has done to my habits!

2

I shall read a poem by your coffin
I shall place myself adjacent to you
And your face will be an inch of pine
From my fingers which will rest
Eloquently in the book's division

How your ancient peers will look
Bewildered
How their eyes will swim with
Modesty

3

This funeral will be the death of me
I mean
The thing hangs over me itself a shroud
I would steal you
I would run away with you
But the mortician has painted your face
And arriving breathless with you
On an urban bankside
Flushed with the thrill of my theft
I would prise off your lid and
You
Oh you would look foolish
As never in life

4

How we staggered in your last hours
How absurdly we fell around
You dying weak
Me never strong
How comically we tottered
I know you would laugh
To hear it described

5

I think you were mine
I think I owned you
Or at least owned what I chose
To think was you
The map of you through which
I drew fierce lines of
Territorial possession
I now must share
I must throw open frontiers
For the day and exchange
With dignitaries gifts of the past
I would like in so much diplomacy
To thrust my hand into your box
And for your dead mouth to snap
Affectionately on my wrist
Old and irregular teeth

Are These the Best of My Life?

Are these the best of my life?
The gulls quarrel
My sons sleep
My shirt is so beautiful on the chair
Like a parchment
Every crease of which is studied

Are these the best of my life?
The surgeon has made a wound
Of my love's belly
And she sleeps in a distant room
To the traffic's hiss
The futile parabola of laughing lights

Are these the best of my life?
A friend has praised me in terms
I could not imitate
And the moon presses its damaged side
To my cheek
An untrustworthy accolyte

Are these the best of my life?
I could want to hold the cool arse
Of a mischievous girl
I could want to hear my mother laugh
Or find safety again as a boy
Sleeps with an animal made of cones

37

The Peterhead Gaol Mutiny of 1987

Here is an historic photograph
A dog has a dog on a chain

Here is a show for the public
The roof is a ramp for mannequins

At the same hour the hooded criminal
Takes the hatless gaoler for a walk

He threatens to beat out his brains
On the slippery slates

How well the dog cringes as if
He had been all his life a cur

How badly the wielder of death
Plays anger it is too demonstrative

One of them is right or neither
One of them is cruel but which

Our sympathy has not been focussed
Since pity will always adhere

To the one about to suffer
No matter how bloody his career

But let's be just

It can't be easy to show complexity
At an angle of 45 degrees

You cannot always choose your stage
The point is to acquire an audience

And in this respect the performance
Must be judged a staggering success

Millions learned how men become dogs
They learned the power of chains

The Tide's Advice

Emulate dead seamen
Rise through flooded floors
And let the current carry you
Through hatches with the escaping air
You will suffer glancing blows but numbly

Follow the routes of the drowned
Who navigate perilous points
Passing between the shallow banks
With unhurried piloting and
Greeting the buoys in their beams
The rocks will slice you but kindly

They have become the substance
And do not dissent
They have permission of the moon
All argument suspended in her pull
Which covers and uncovers
The same wreck
The same fragment of industry or idleness

Be three-quarters hid
From the gull's exacting nerves
Concede an eye to its appetite
And at the end of long passages lodge
Silently in the rain-pocked bay
Or fix between the piles
Of strenuous harbours
A puzzle
An escapee
A non-contributor

The Moon's Advice

Be hard in the body
Make every granite bear
The scars of your passage
Go into the repetitive field
And call up the wild
With the horn of your hands

State your brevity
Will not go unremarked

Be what the lunatic would be
If she were allowed to love
Refuse all condolences
And in the midst of laughter
Take your coat and leave

Find satisfaction
In the glacier's inexorable advance
Its crack in the night
Its hunger for warm seas
Dragging in its bed all hindrances

Seethe at imbalance
And at the balancer's ineptitude
And abandoned by all who wanted you
But could only tolerate the part of you
Lie out
Dying out
Alone
Your applause
Will wake
A single child in its mundane room

The Diminishing Authority of Heroic Teachers

Perfectly rotund his phrases
Make their leisurely excursion
Of the adolescent hall

His hair a silver storm of calculated
Neglect

Abandoned concepts flock to his shoulder
Perch
Preen and
Shit

Once they winged through learned pages
Now they pluck the colours out
Of their own chests

How thick the floor is
Underneath the desk
A guano of the rarely quoted
And reputations hardly dead

He dreamed his jaw would plough
A trireme bow
Through their placidity
Instead
They rise a park of pigeons
On his last full stop

Today their eyes did not adore
Today they were islands of insouciance
There was no roar
Of the hundred throats approving

He must telephone his mistress
He must put his mouth to her breast

Her knees are beech
Her shoulders are yew

How completely she reassures
It is as if she knew
His splendour was unjustly obscured

He stabs the meal
He goads the bread
Calling them a doleful generation
And in the bed
His acts of love are parodic
Even she fails to conceal

Why Not

How angry you are
How your eyes are cloaked in suspicion
How you fear the male
While shortening your skirt

You were abandoned in the seventh month
And your child dreams your days
Of rage
Sleeping inverted
Your eyes are bleached of hope
And the reluctant smile is a red cave
Tenanted by the fugitive

It is dishonest to pretend
Your tension does not excite me
More even
Than your proffered arse
But how much of other life
You bring into the bedroom
Even nakedness is stained
And resignation mutters its
Prior knowledge beneath
The cry of love

Certainly a man would have to earn
His peace with you
Infinitely patient he would take
So many blows and in return
You'd make a small place for him
An animal whose warmth absorbs the idle hand.

The Gaoler's Ache for the Nearly Dead

(Fotheringhay, 1587)

Up the stairs then you have stagnated here
Shedding the regal manner by degrees

Up now I should not like to coerce you
We should both lose face and they are waiting

With the racing pulse of the recently rich who know
Their titles are not safe until you bleed

I was disposed to feel the power of the fallen
Even without your reputation for clandestine love

Did you not feel my little kindnesses and cruelties
The spite alternating with excessive services?

These are the symptoms of desire in the unequal
The distorted shape of longing in the powerless

I catch the flash of heels under your hems
Keenly as the predator spots life among the bracken

And the friction of your pleats is a straw fire
In the uncommon silence of this passage

All this has been rehearsed
A maid stood in for you reluctant and yet grinning

How pleasant to play the passing infamy
And sing your life again in the certain evening

She could not kneel like you however
You kneel as none ever did folding your life like a stool

And swiftly leaning to the block deprive their
Trawling eyes of your last look a sexual trophy

Or a cure for the palsy
Your fear has all drained into your hands

Which are a knot of knuckle on your stooping back
A pale crab writhing on black crêpe

Give them nothing yell your complaints
And I will fight them for your clothes

I will spoil by my clamour for your relics
The dignity new classes smile at in the old

Caxais, the Prison

(Attempts Towards a Carvalhoad)

I enter here bemused
I have discovered this faculty with years
I enter with a smile draped
Over my face like a hawk's hood
A convivial thing to deflect malice
My shoes ring music from the floors
Caxais

I am no longer the hero of Portugal
The relief nourishes my bones
And my hair is thicker from
The extinction of my reputation
Which was like a cloth waved
A simple action and repetitive
Caxais

I toppled the dictator
Springing a crowd from silence
As shaving cream spurts into foam
The million mouths of gratitude
Slobbered my jeep's wheels
I restored dead men to their tables
And brought laughter home
Caxais

Thank you
This is one of the better cells
And far above the water level
Thank you
This view might comfort me
Showing as it does the little boats
And the rhythm of the fisher's engines
As he carves his wake in the night
Will sometimes madden
And sometimes console
His routine perfect and yet vile
I shall wish him to drown some nights
But miss his return to the mooring

Thank you
For pen and paper and certain books
Though only the thoroughly depraved
Or wholly contemplative can move me now
These titles have the odour of
Moderate hopes
Classic expectations
Reconciliations and the like
Perhaps you do this to torture me
Whilst pretending to be kind?
I am deeply suspicious of a decent motive
And always the food excites in me
A sense of imminent death

Thank you
For restraining me
My impatience with those I once embraced
My contempt for the innocent is now such
I should inflict
The whole catalogue of old atrocity
I am not without this sensibility
I am not so theoretical
I cannot taste the pleasure of the arbitrary act
Keep me tight or I will
If not participate inspire
Acts whose notoriety will mock
The pity I first felt for suffering

Caxais
Once I came here like a god
And godlike went into the deepest dark
With flashlights and a few troops
Coloured from colonial campaigns
Like old immortals we groped down hell
I freed the living and unslung the dead
From moats and cisterns where they
Stood a crop of sodden heads
Among which like the tenders of
Watercress in its tinkling beds
The gaolers rowed out for confessions

Caxais
The sea had been invited in
And ebbed between iron pillars
Lapping the lips of the intransigent
How little did they think me possible
They did not dare to dream me
Parting them from death
Carvalho
Renegade
Restorer of impossible and ruptured loves
Bringer of the sunlight
Carvalho
The thrower down of doors which drifted
Through our laughter to Atlantic waves

My picture hung in windows
Flapped from the café walls
I knew the transience of this
But would not be unadored
Or show I smarted from exaggeration
Not loving them
But not depriving them
My holiness prevailed for forty weeks
Of change

And here I ought
In contemplation of such actors of the past
To have resigned
And on a balcony provided by the state
Watched bonfires light the curve
Of celebrating arses
And slept late
Carvalho who drew the blind on
Misery's excess

But I laid thought on thought
Shifting the ground of torture from
The malice of a bloody room
To unequal labour and poverty's sublingual hiss
And finding gaols in factories and fields
Caxais with its ponds
Flowed in all our relations
Are we not in a chamber with each other
And some bound?

You could not begin and simply cease
You could not demolish and not reconstruct
Or see the return of the guilty
In suits of a different cloth
Carvalho could not call off the
Hounds of his imagination
Carvalho was not wise enough
To let the casual opportunist
Govern with approximations

Caxais
I am here again!
Someone I inspired shot a proprietor
Caxais
Your worn stairs are nearly affectionate!
Someone I influenced threw bombs into a bank
Tearing the arms off a beggar
Who worked the taxi rank
Caxais

I have my following
But the mass is happy to account me dead
This room
This table
Are perfectly kind
Not offering hope
And the tin clock ticking draws away my life
No mutiny will open these doors twice
Or random shots burst in the
Ears of the amazed
Caxais
I shall become a gargoyle
Whose dangling tongue drips rainwater
On crowds

Lullabies for the Impatient

First Lullaby

I report the decay of ideals
To the hungry minded

I narrate the slipping of faiths
To the wild with impatience

The
Rags
Of
Programmes

The
Threadbare
Fabric
Of
Deals

THE SPEED WITH WHICH BOOKS DRAIN OF COLOUR
AND SLOGANS TAKE THE MEANING OF THE WALL

For which we breathe a scarcely audible thanks
As banned religionists mutter their amen
In abbeys stacked with straw and tanks

*

The old woman seized my hand
I might have been her son

The old woman spoke an unknown tongue
I might have been her husband

Rushing me along
I might have been her aged mother

So impatient was she
I might have been the insane product
Of her single night of love

And consigning the police to the gutter
She led me to the door of her delight

The barred cathedral
She had warrened
Like a rat

I report the persistence of myths
In the banned heart

I narrate the love of the mystical
In the obsessively practical

The poor livers who discover properties
In the halls of the recorded dead

She laps the memorials to the disappeared
Wars ago they were her peers

She clings to things so barely tolerated
They are without taint

Things dignified by the implacable
Hostility of states
Which in their ardour shone with
A different depravity
Bishops of the Empire
Bronzes of disbanded regiments
The flagrant nakedness of mechants' wives
These
She rinses in her breath

It is only a matter of waiting
The theorists die in sanatoria
And the young have long ceased to tell their texts

*

Second Lullaby

You act as if speech itself could not be trusted
As if articulation swung like chains from idle cranes
Slack in a wet sky

You prefer silence in the cacophony
You idealize the downturned mouth
And condemn laughter as collective fear

Tell me about your children then
They at least know little
And find pleasure in trowelling words

Or your garden with its night time odours
There was much kissing in that little space
And the woman next door aroused you

I am so happy to see you and have opened
Not a single bottle but a cask to welcome you
Everthing was brutal in this field once

But now we have raised ten harvests
I will do the talking for you
But look! Still you sit on the edge of your chair!

*

Third Lullaby

Finding the rebel had killed his enemy
Not swiftly as if death were a necessity
But slowly as if it painted his day
You flinched

Finding the spokesman for the poor
Was a liar who loved not only their applause
But the better view he obtained from their backs
You shrank

Finding the designer of the new society
Beat a man for casting a glance at his wife
And wept a week for her infidelity
You frowned

Torturers
Lawyers
Fetishists

Yet you require heroes to purify life!

Remember the saints slaughter
Without pause for the sunset

*

Fourth Lullaby

You think we are governed by thieves?
Not for the first time

Old thieves are best
Like horticulturalists
They know you must
Leave something on the bough

But these!

You think the point has been reached?
The future may not be better

Peace might be worse than war
Harmony worse than dissonance
The new class full of anger
An anger worse than indolence

It's possible

You do not care for this proposition?
Yes
Down with the pessimists!

Whoever asked an old woman
If she would welcome a riot?
As for the infants
They affirm everything
In their tantrums

*

Fifth Lullaby

Your room is very tight tonight
And all the things that you believe
Are not believed by others

Your letters have gone unremarked
And the woman who offered you her life
Has shown herself immune to your neglect

Down at the water's edge your idol
Prepares to abandon his post
He has rebuked the waves to no effect

This time is parsimonious with hope
Electing the weakest as the bearer
Of unappetising truth

How neglectfully it sows bravery
How inequitable its distribution
Of the faculty of disbelief

Go to the kind mirror on the door
And greet your whole self naked
Your shoulder has only to recover

And your hip regain its power
For you to exhibit in your stance
The pagan attitude of endurance

63

The poor beat out their losses on bins
They cannot shift their axis by eruption
And the rich go by with their animal cry

How clean your limbs are in the
Artificial light and your phallus
Rehearses its impetuosity

*

Sixth Lullaby

Simple rain puts flinching in their faces
Shrapnel from the sky could not wring them
More furtive in the jaw

Compare the mongrel

Whose wet body in an ecstasy of writhing
Strings itself about a stinking joint

No distraction from pure appetite

You shall be so undivided and unshrinking
So gnawing and so blind to consequence

You shall laugh with the bride whose whiteness
Her groom has not the confidence to fling
You shall wade in her clouds of netting

You mongrel over the town's hills
You impossible to trap

You shall turn at the high corner
With the dog's unfathomable stillness

The stray's one moment of knowledge
It lives only for itself

*

Seventh Lullaby

You are not mistaken the sky is yellow
This is the breath of talented liars
Clinging to the floor of the clouds

You are not mistaken the walls are warped
By the ground renouncing its rules
And the smell which spoils the air
Is hope's sickness spreading down the stair

Goodbye then
Simple satisfactions of immutable laws
Portable kits of blame

Goodbye
The dead dictator's notes on popular control
And the old poet's memoirs of his circle's bliss

The new predator is not aloof
He is not spoiled by art
Preferring beachwear to the unkind leather

How well he whistles sentiments such as
WE ARE ALL IN THIS TOGETHER
How simply he articulates our needs
I AM YOU AND YOU ARE ME

With some lies it is not sensible to disagree

Be seen in black therefore
It is becoming in the sallow
As blood is excellent against the yellow
Of monks' robes

You too will bleed

Prance in black
It was ever the unfair colour
Bestowing dignity on the ill-willed
And repeating night's
Cheap repertoire of fears

You too will oppress

Stir your coffee with one eye on the door
A frame of unexpected love
Or the escape from unprovoked eruption

Learn the art of walking slowly
In the street
The beggars will recognize you
And despite the kindness in your eye
They will stare at their feet
Surrendering habitual impertinence
To your priestly manner

While she who hesitated to embrace you
Will feel herself aged by her abstinence

*

Eighth Lullaby

It's true you have been overlooked
Certainly the victim of conspiracy
I must acknowledge there are those
Who for the most contemptible of reasons
Have placed obstacles in your path
I too have heard the baying laugh
Of those who scorned the ground you gained
And sang your very natural errors
In the public place.
As for your obscure origins
Who could deny the wound this makes?
In some ways you were too much loved
In others a terrible coldness rained.
In such a complex personality as yours
We understand ingratitude is only pain.
As for the climate of the time
It shrivvels all the fine ideas
Things never were more hostile
Even in the laughing years.
Beauty has set cold coins on her eyes
And where passion was prized
The idol of accumulation stands.
How fortunate that women love you so!
In their dilated eyes you see
Yourself suitably enlarged
A black figure of heroic lassitude
Hurting their throats with your hands.

You Came!

You came!
And I thought she will capitulate to his despair
She will pity the penitent hang of his head

You came!

And I thought she will gather the scattered pack of days
Into a frail house for a convalescent love

You came!

Look how the single star throbs on the evening's rim
As a rebuke to my poor faith

We travel from opposing ends of this loud place
Weaving among the routine and the accidental

Steering a pliable course between the supplicating
And the criminal

Shunning the deserving
Unswerving for the stranded
Nimble to evade the cruel

How implacable our explorations are
We have moved mapless beyond shame
To arrive at this magnetic place

Your breath conceals me like a mother's
From imaginary fears
And your round knee is warm as
The polished woods of ancient stairs

History Poem

My ally
Down in the country
Has taken to planting again
And talks fondly of restoring himself
To his wife

My ally
Up in the city
Is looking for new phrases to describe
The apparently irrational behaviour of the
Electorate

I hear the shovel striking flints
I hear the howl of the abused typewriter

At a certain hour
All three of us
Must yield to sleep